BRUNO
THE
PRETZEL
MAN

BRUNO THE PRETZEL MAN

by Edward E. Davis
illustrated by Marc Simont

Harper & Row, Publishers

Library of Congress Cataloging in Publication Data
Davis, Edward E., 1939–
    Bruno the pretzel man.

    Summary: A pretzel vendor discovers that he is just
as happy, and important, as the businessmen who buy
his wife's delicious pretzels.
    [1. Pretzels.—Fiction.   2. Peddlers and peddling
—Fiction.   3. New York (N.Y.)—Fiction]   I. Simont,
Marc, ill.   II. Title.
PZ7.D2874Br 1984   [E]   84-47630
ISBN 0-06-021398-1
ISBN 0-06-021399-X (lib. bdg.)

Designed by Al Cetta
1 2 3 4 5 6 7 8 9 10
First Edition

For Nancy, with love and thanks
for so many good years

BRUNO
THE
PRETZEL
MAN

ONE

Bruno the pretzel man had a small pushcart with a warm charcoal grill on top that kept his pretzels nice and fresh. Every morning Bruno would wake up, get out of bed, look out the window, stretch his body, and say, "It's a fine day to go out and sell pretzels."

Bruno's wife, who was always in the kitchen baking pretzels by this time, would say, "Oh, Bruno, you always think it's a fine day to sell pretzels even when it's raining so hard that no one bothers to stop and buy." Bruno could not deny this, because it was true.

But Bruno hadn't always sold pretzels, and his wife, whom many people called Mrs. Bruno even though her name was Esmerelda, hadn't always baked them.

Bruno was born in a country far across the ocean. When he was a young boy, his mother and father thought it would be a good idea for him to learn a trade. They sent him to live with a tailor, so that after a few years he would be good enough to be a tailor's apprentice, and after a few more years he would be a tailor himself and teach others.

Bruno was a good boy and did what his parents thought best, but no matter how hard he tried, he wasn't good at tailoring. His seams were crooked, his stitches were uneven, and his hems fell down. Even worse, he once managed to stitch two pant legs together on a suit that belonged to a very good customer.

Although the tailor liked Bruno very much, he often said, "Bruno, Bruno, what should I do with you? I promised your parents I would make you into a tailor, but the way things are now, you are just another mouth to feed."

Bruno liked the tailor very much, but had to agree that everything the tailor said was true.

Bruno's parents tried making him an apprentice to a shoemaker, a barber, and a farmer, but Bruno only ended up making two left shoes instead of pairs, cutting his customers' hair unevenly, and not being able to catch the pigs.

"Even the army would not take you, Bruno," his father said. But they all found out that was not true, for when Bruno's parents decided to move to America, the army did take Bruno.

Life in the army was pleasant enough for the

young man, now an American. All he did was drive a jeep with an important general in it. The general would tell Bruno where to drive and Bruno would go just where the general asked him to. He didn't drive too fast or too slow. "Bruno," the general would say, "you drive just right. Not like my last three drivers. You will go far in the army."

But Bruno did not want to go far in the army, and when it was time for his enlistment to end, he decided to move to New York to seek his fortune.

"New York is a big city," Bruno's father said. "What will you do there? You have no skills. You only know how to drive a general."

Bruno only smiled and said, "I will find something wonderful to do that will make my heart sing with joy."

When Bruno came to New York, he got a job as a taxi driver. Then he found a small apartment on the second floor of a nice brick building. Bruno drove his taxi for a few weeks, but the more he drove, the less he liked doing it. It just wasn't the same as driving an important general around. His customers always wanted to go too fast. And because New York was so big, Bruno often got lost. Bruno was amazed to find that many of his customers did not know how to go where they were going.

"Why do you want to go to King's Highway," Bruno once asked one of his customers, "if you don't even know where it is?"

"Mind your own business and keep your eyes on the road," the man snapped back at Bruno.

Bruno decided to quit and try to find what it was that he really wanted to do, something that would make his heart sing with joy.

Bruno walked around New York for many days, looking at all the store windows and the people rushing by. They always seemed to be in such a hurry. "I wish I had something to be in a hurry for," Bruno would say to himself.

Wherever he walked Bruno would be sure to stop and buy a pretzel from a street vendor, for Bruno liked to eat pretzels more than anything else in the world. In fact, he began to keep careful notes of the pretzels he had eaten. After a while Bruno's pretzel notebook looked like this:

52nd Street and Lexington Avenue: pretzel too hard, January 14th.

Mulberry and Broome streets: pretzel had too much salt, January 15th.

34th Street and Sixth Avenue: pretzel too cold and now costs a nickel more than it did last week. What is the world coming to? January 16th.

Each day Bruno would tell himself, "Today I will find the perfect pretzel." On some of those days Bruno thought, "Today I will find something to do that will make my heart sing with joy." But each day Bruno would come home disappointed.

Some days Bruno would go uptown and other days he would go downtown. Sometimes he would go to the east side and other times to the west side. After a while Bruno knew every pretzel vendor in New York by name, but he could not find a pretzel that was like the kind he had in his old home town when he was a boy.

TWO

But one day a strange thing happened. Bruno was walking along the sidewalk, thinking about all the pretzels he had eaten and didn't think were very good, when he turned onto a street he had never before been on. It was a fine wide street called 57th Street.

How is it, you may ask, that in all this wandering Bruno had never been on such an important street? Why, the answer is simple. New York is such a big city that it is almost impossible for anyone to be on all the streets.

As Bruno was walking on 57th Street thinking about pretzels, he heard a voice crying out, "Pretzels, pretzels, freshly baked pretzels." Bruno stopped and looked but he saw no pretzel cart. He looked again and saw a young woman standing in front of a jewelry store, holding two large shopping bags filled with pretzels.

Although his heart was not really in it, Bruno bought a pretzel from the woman and took a bite. He took only three steps and he stopped, turned around, and jumped into the air, shouting, "Why this is the best pretzel I have ever tasted!"

People passing by on the street were so aston-ished that they stopped whatever they were doing to look at this strange man eating a pretzel and jumping up and down. The poor woman who sold the pretzel to Bruno was so embarrassed, she immediately picked up her shopping bags and tried to walk away.

But Bruno would not let her, for his heart began to sing with joy. He immediately bought a second pretzel and began eating it before he had finished the first. Soon Bruno and the woman with the shopping bags were surrounded by people staring at Bruno, who was holding a pretzel in each hand and jumping up and down. As the people crowded around, some began to buy pretzels and soon some of them, too, began jumping up and down after a few bites.

It wasn't long before the block was filled with people holding pretzels in their hands and jumping up and down. They spilled out into the street, and the drivers of the cars began blowing their horns. In a few minutes traffic was backed up for blocks, and some of the drivers left their cars to see what was going on.

"In all my life," Bruno said to the young woman, "never have I tasted pretzels such as these. Every day I go out and eat a pretzel. This day I have eaten two. I never eat two," he said.

Esmerelda, for that was the young woman's name, was so pleased by Bruno's opinion of her pretzels, she forgot she was embarrassed and gave Bruno a big smile.

Esmerelda told Bruno that every morning she got up early to bake her pretzels and then she would put them in shopping bags and sell them on the street. Although she knew her pretzels were good, she was beginning to lose hope because she sold so few.

"But no one can see them in your shopping bags," Bruno said. "You must have a pretzel cart like others do."

"But I have no idea how to do that," she said. "I am good at baking pretzels, but not at carts."

"But it is easy," Bruno said, for having seen every pretzel vendor in New York, he knew exactly what Esmerelda should do. But the more Bruno tried to explain, the more confused she became.

It did not take Bruno and Esmerelda long to decide that she would bake the pretzels and Bruno would sell them from a cart.

By the end of the following week Bruno purchased a secondhand cart with his savings left over from when he was a taxi driver. Soon after that

Bruno got a license from the City of New York to sell pretzels.

One month to the day after Bruno and Esmerelda met, Bruno wheeled his pretzel cart to the exact spot where he had first seen her at 57th Street and Fifth Avenue and began to sell pretzels.

Four weeks after that, Bruno and Esmerelda were married. Esmerelda's parents liked Bruno very much and were also happy to have Esmerelda's room for her younger sister, Margarita.

Bruno's parents, who lived in Buffalo, New York, came all the way to New York City for the wedding.

"Well, Bruno," his father said, "it looks like you have found something useful in life."

"Yes," Bruno said. "This is the thing that makes my heart sing with joy."

THREE

Esmerelda was very much like Bruno. Her parents
used to say, "Esmerelda, what can you do? You are
not clever like other girls. You do not sew well,
you have nothing to teach, how can you ever find a
husband?"

"Phooey on husbands," Esmerelda would say.
"I am happy just baking my pretzels." But some
nights when she went to bed, Esmerelda knew that
wasn't so. The day after Esmerelda met Bruno, she
did not say, "Phooey on husbands." Her failure to
say this did not escape the attention of Esmerelda's
mother, who later that evening said to Esmerelda's
father, "Something is up with our Esmerelda. She
has met a man."

"You are dreaming," he replied. "She cares for
nothing but her pretzels."

"You will see, you will see," Esmerelda's mother
said.

Bruno and Esmerelda lived in Bruno's small
second-floor apartment and were very happy.
Every morning Esmerelda would get up early and

start to bake her delicious pretzels. As the smell floated into their small bedroom Bruno would get up, look out the window, stretch his body, and say, "It's a fine day to go out and sell pretzels."

Their neighbors loved to wake up to the smell of freshly baked pretzels. Every morning they would knock on the door to buy pretzels. Bruno and Esmerelda were proud that their neighbors were their first customers.

Every morning Bruno would pull his cart from the basement and dust it off so the sign, BRUNO, stood out clearly. At first the sign said BRUNO THE PRETZEL MAN, but one of his customers, a man in a fine gray suit, said, "Why do you bother with that? It is obvious you are a pretzel man. You are selling pretzels. If you were selling hats, would you have a sign that said BRUNO THE HAT MAN?"

"But I know nothing of hats," Bruno replied, "so I would never have a sign that said BRUNO THE HAT MAN."

"That is not the point," the man said.

"Then I do not understand why you asked," Bruno replied. But the more he thought about it, the more he thought that the man might be right.

"He always walks by in a hurry," Bruno told Esmerelda one night. "He has a fine gray suit and talks to important people."

"All those things are nice," Esmerelda replied, "but that doesn't mean he is right. But if it makes you happy to change the sign, you should do it. We will still sell the same number of pretzels." And that is how Bruno the pretzel man became just plain Bruno.

Every Monday, Tuesday, Wednesday, Thursday, and Friday, Bruno would stand at the corner of 57th Street and Fifth Avenue in New York City with his cart. On rainy days he had an umbrella, and always his small charcoal heater would keep the pretzels warm.

Every night he would come home and tell Esmerelda about his customers, especially the man in the fine gray suit.

"Imagine such a thing," he said to Esmerelda, "such important people buying our pretzels."

"But why shouldn't they?" Esmerelda asked. "Our pretzels are the best. And who is to say that a man is more important than you just because he wears a nice suit?"

"Of course he is important," Bruno replied. "I am just a pretzel seller."

"But you are my pretzel seller," Esmerelda said. "And I won't hear another word about such things."

FOUR

As time passed, people began to know Bruno and they bought more and more pretzels from him. Bruno and Esmerelda were not rich, but they had enough for their needs. And although they had no children, they hoped for the day when they might. Some days Bruno would stand by his cart thinking that one day he could change the sign to read BRUNO AND SON or BRUNO AND DAUGHTER. Other days all Bruno could think about was when it would be time for lunch so he could eat his pretzel.

Every day Bruno ate a pretzel for lunch. Never two and never anything else. Always one pretzel. He ate it slowly and chewed it thoroughly to enjoy every last crumb. When he finished he would wipe his mouth carefully with a napkin, crumple the napkin and throw it into his trash basket, and say to himself, "I am truly a lucky man. I have a wonderful wife, and every day I eat the best pretzel in the world. I want for nothing and my heart sings with joy."

But as the days passed, Bruno became more and more curious about the men who hurried by in their nice suits, especially the man in the fine gray suit. Many times, the man would stop to buy a pretzel from Bruno. Often he would speak of things that Bruno did not understand, important things.

One day the man stopped by with a friend to buy a pretzel. "Just on the way to lunch," he said to Bruno. "Nothing like a fresh Bruno pretzel to tide us over. What do you do when you're not selling pretzels?" he asked.

"Why, what a question," Bruno replied. "I am always selling pretzels. That is my job."

"How will you ever become important if you spend all your time selling pretzels?" the man asked. "You have to look around. There is opportunity everywhere, but you will not find it behind a pretzel cart.

"Look at me," the man continued. "I have an important job in the stock market. You can't do that from a pretzel cart. You don't even sell your pretzels the right way. Don't you know that you have the best pretzels in New York? People will pay more for your pretzels. It's an economic fact of life, Bruno," the man said. "You should charge a nickel more, maybe even a dime."

"But I charge a fair price," Bruno said. "I am not a greedy man. I do not need more money."

"It's a dog-eat-dog world, Bruno," the man said. "Do it to them, before they do it to you." And he walked away.

That night after Bruno went home, he didn't say much to Esmerelda. He kept thinking about what the man in the fine gray suit had said. Surely he was right, Bruno thought. Could such an important man be wrong? He always seemed so sure of himself. "How can I become an important person from behind a pretzel cart?" Bruno thought.

The more Bruno thought about what the man in the fine gray suit had said, the more he wondered how he could get around and see what was what. He could move his pretzel cart, but that didn't seem to be such a good idea. How would his customers find him? And then he would still be behind his pretzel cart. No. There simply had to be another way . . . a way that he could get away from the pretzel cart.

If only he had someone who could watch his cart for him at lunchtime, so that he could walk around for an hour or so. But how could he find such a person?

The more he thought about his problem, the

sadder he became, until his heart no longer sang with joy. Every day Bruno wheeled his pretzel cart to the same spot and watched the people walking by, always hurrying. They all looked important to Bruno even though he no longer knew what he meant by important. He knew only that he was not, and the more he thought about it, the sadder he felt.

FIVE

One evening when Bruno came home, Esmerelda was reading the newspaper.

"Just look at all this," she said. "There is so little news and so many ads. Ads for this and ads for that. Ads for the stores and ads for jobs."

"But that is the way it always is," Bruno said. And suddenly it came to him. He knew just how he would find someone to watch his cart. He would place an ad in the newspaper. After Esmerelda had gone to bed, Bruno took out a piece of paper and a pencil and he wrote this ad:

Wanted: Someone to watch my pretzel cart at lunchtime. See Bruno at 57th St. and Fifth Ave.

The next day, after Bruno had sold his last pretzel, he walked to the newspaper office and gave the clerk his ad. The ad cost Bruno two dollars.

Two days later, a young man came up to Bruno and said, "I am looking for Bruno." He showed Bruno the ad from the newspaper.

"I am Bruno," Bruno replied. "Have a pretzel."

"This," the young man said, "is the best pretzel I have ever tasted in my life. I would be very pleased to watch your pretzel cart while you have lunch."

"I can pay you one dollar an hour," Bruno said. "Is that all right?"

"One dollar an hour is fine," the man said. "My name is David, and I just love your pretzels."

As they talked, the man in the fine gray suit came by with his friends to buy pretzels. "How's it going, Bruno?" he asked. "Did you ever decide to go out in the world and look around?"

"I did," Bruno exclaimed. "Look, here is David, and he will watch my pretzel cart while I have lunch with you and your friends tomorrow." Then, turning to David, he said, "You see, I am on my way to becoming someone very important."

The man in the fine gray suit didn't say anything. He just bought a pretzel, smiled at Bruno, and walked away.

"See how important he is," Bruno said to David, "and what important friends he has. Every day they come here and buy a pretzel."

"But why shouldn't they?" David asked. "You have the finest pretzels in all of New York."

"That's it exactly," Bruno cried. And he told David the whole story of how he saw Esmerelda with the shopping bags and how all the traffic on 57th Street couldn't move and how, that day, he had two pretzels. They stood there slowly eating their pretzels, and then David told Bruno about how he had tried different jobs, never liking any of them.

"I was fired from a shoe store once," David said, "because I said that the shoes didn't fit the customer well. The manager was furious."

"But it's always important to tell the truth," Bruno said, taking another bite of his pretzel.

"That's it exactly," David said, chewing his pretzel. "My parents told me always to tell the truth."

"I once sewed two pant legs together when I was apprenticed to a tailor," Bruno said, biting into another pretzel.

"When I worked in the toy store," David said, chewing another pretzel, "I packed in a box of crayons with each coloring book. Whoever heard of a coloring book without crayons? But the manager fired me."

"You were right, you know," Bruno replied, taking another pretzel.

And the more they talked, the more pretzels they ate. Bruno told David about how he used to drive the general and David told Bruno about how he used to be a cook. Then Bruno told David about how he used to drive a taxi and then David told

Bruno about how he went on a diet to become a jockey, but then found out that he didn't like bouncing up and down on the horses. And each time they told a story, they each ate another pretzel.

The time passed so quickly, neither realized how late it was getting, until finally Bruno said, "Why, it's almost dark. Esmerelda will wonder what has happened."

And that said, Bruno insisted that David come home with him to meet Esmerelda. Now in New York, you can't take a pretzel cart on the bus or on the subway train, and 57th Street and Fifth Avenue was a long way from where Bruno lived. The only thing they could do was walk. Bruno didn't mind such a long walk since it was good exercise and he was used to it. David said he didn't mind either, but about halfway to Bruno's house, David's feet began to hurt. Not only that, but both of them had eaten so many pretzels that they began to get stomachaches.

By the time they walked in the door, they could hardly stand up. David didn't know if his feet hurt more than his stomach, but Esmerelda said that it didn't matter and made them both go to bed, Bruno in his bed and David on the couch in the living room.

SIX

Bruno and David woke up the next morning to the wonderful smell of Esmerelda's fresh pretzels. During breakfast, Bruno told Esmerelda that David would watch the cart.

"But Bruno," Esmerelda said, "why all of a sudden do you have to go somewhere for lunch?"

"Can't a man have a change of scenery now and then?" Bruno asked.

Esmerelda decided to say nothing more, and besides, she liked David very much. But after they both left that morning, she said to herself, "Something is up with my Bruno."

Bruno could hardly wait until it was time for lunch. He kept glancing at the large clock on a nearby storefront and once exclaimed, "Will it never be lunchtime?"

"Today I will begin to be important," Bruno told David. "I will have lunch with the man in the fine gray suit and his friends. You will see."

"But Bruno," David began to say, and then said nothing at all. "We will see what is what," he thought as he ate a pretzel.

At 12:15 the man in the fine gray suit arrived with his friends. After he bought a pretzel and took a bite, he turned to Bruno and said, "Well, Bruno, ready for lunch? We are going to Jean-Claude's, the best French restaurant in town."

"Lead on," Bruno cried with great excitement. "I am ready!" And turning to give David a big smile, he walked off with the man in the fine gray suit and his friends.

Bruno had never been in such a splendid restaurant. There were starched white linen tablecloths on all the tables and real silverware. All the men and women in the restaurant were beautifully dressed except Bruno. Suddenly, he began to look at his checked jacket and worn leather cap and he felt ashamed.

As if he could read Bruno's mind, one of the men said, "Don't worry, Bruno, they'll think you're an important author." All the men laughed when he said that, and Bruno tried to laugh, too, but he felt too nervous. This was unlike any restaurant he had ever been in. He had only been to cafeterias with Esmerelda, and here there were no trays and lines. "Why should we go out to eat?" Esmerelda always said. "I cook better than any restaurant." And, of course, Bruno agreed because it was true.

[37]

Now they were approached by a man in a black tuxedo, and Bruno began to get so nervous that the palms of his hands began to sweat and his knees started shaking. "If I don't sit down soon," Bruno thought, "I am going to faint. Better still, maybe I should just get out of here."

But before he could say or do anything, the man in the fine gray suit said, "My usual table," to the man in the black tuxedo. And suddenly they were all walking to a large table right in the middle of the room where everyone could see them.

When the menu came, Bruno couldn't understand a word of it since it was all in French. "What if I order the wrong thing," he thought. Although Bruno's knees had stopped shaking, his palms were still sweating and he suddenly realized that he had to go to the bathroom. He glanced around the room, but saw no signs anywhere. The more he looked, the worse he had to go. Finally, he said to the man in the fine gray suit, "Is there a bathroom here?" The man in the fine gray suit pointed to a stairway that led downstairs.

When Bruno was finished in the bathroom, a man in a uniform jumped up quickly and turned on the water faucets at one of the sinks. Bruno wasn't sure just what to do, so he washed his hands. Then the man handed him a towel and while Bruno was

drying his hands, the man brushed his jacket with a small straw broom. Bruno's knees started trembling again. Was he supposed to give this man money? Would the man be offended if Bruno gave him something? Would he be offended if Bruno did not give him something?

Bruno decided to take a chance and he reached into his pocket and gave the man a nickel. The man stood there staring at it, his body blocking the door, and then gave the nickel back to Bruno. As the man stepped aside to let Bruno pass, Bruno thought, "I have made a mistake. I shouldn't have given him money. He was offended."

As Bruno climbed the stairs back to the main floor, his knees began trembling worse than ever, and his hands that he had just washed were sweating even more than before.

By the time Bruno sat down, everyone at his table had a small plate of salad with dressing.

"Bruno, we ordered a salad for you to start. Hope you don't mind," one of the men said.

Bruno was so grateful that they had ordered for him, he lunged for the salad plate with his fork and knocked over the glass of water at his elbow.

Instantly the man in the black tuxedo appeared with two waiters, their arms filled with large cloth napkins. As the waiters began mopping up the

water from the table, the man in the tuxedo said, "Don't worry about a thing. It happens all the time."

But Bruno was so upset that he could scarcely remember how or why he had come to Jean-Claude's. All he could think of was how to get out quickly. He looked around for the exit, but his view was blocked by two more waiters who came with large plates of food.

"We ordered the specialty of the house for you, Bruno," the man in the fine gray suit said.

Bruno felt he should eat some of the food because he didn't want to insult the cook's feelings. But after two or three bites, he didn't know what it was and he didn't like the thick yellow sauce that covered it.

"Well, Bruno," one of the men said, "what do you think of the market?"

"But I never go to the market," Bruno said. "Esmerelda does all the shopping." The men at the table all burst out laughing.

"Well then," the man said, "what do you think of the Mideast crisis?"

"Is it a crisis?" Bruno asked. "Oh, well then, there's nothing to be done, is there?" Bruno replied, not knowing what else to say. He really didn't understand anything these men were talking about.

He hated the food. He hated the starched white linen tablecloths and he hated the way the man in the black tuxedo looked at him when he asked for a glass of milk to go with the pretzel that he pulled out of his pocket when everyone else ordered dessert. He was sure that everyone in the restaurant was staring at him. He couldn't wait to get back to his pretzel cart.

When the bill came, the man in the fine gray suit reached over, took it in his hand, and simply signed his name on the back without even looking at it! At that, the other men at the table all got up and pushed back their chairs. Bruno reached in his pocket for some money because he wanted to pay his share, but the man in the fine gray suit just waved it away with his hand. "My treat, Bruno," he said. "One day when you are important, you can buy me lunch at your favorite place."

SEVEN

When Bruno got back to the pretzel cart, he was unusually quiet. "How was lunch, Bruno?" David asked. "What did you talk about? How was the food?" But the more questions David asked, the more quiet Bruno became, until he wouldn't say anything. He did not even notice when his regular customers came to buy pretzels. When the last pretzel was sold, Bruno looked at David and said, "Jean-Claude's is not the right place for me. Tomorrow will be different."

The next day Bruno went to lunch alone at a coffee shop on 58th Street. When Bruno sat down on an empty stool, there behind the counter was one of his customers.

"Well, Bruno, what a nice surprise," the man said.

"That's it exactly," Bruno began to say, but before he could finish his sentence, the man slapped a menu down in front of Bruno and walked away. The atmosphere in the coffee shop was more to Bruno's liking than Jean-Claude's. Bruno didn't feel nervous or upset, but he still felt alone and unimportant. The man behind the counter was too busy serving customers to talk to Bruno, and when he took his order, he didn't even look at him. After Bruno ate his sandwich, he took his pretzel out of his pocket and began to eat that, too. But the manager came over and said, "Hey, no bringing your own food in here. What's the matter with you, you crazy or something?" Then the manager told Bruno to hurry up because people were waiting in line for the stools.

As he walked out of the coffee shop, Bruno thought, "I am nothing to all these people. No one said anything to me. I am not important."

And he stood there on the sidewalk thinking for such a long time that a policeman came by and told him to move on and stop loitering. Bruno immediately recognized the policeman. Ever since he had set up his cart, the policeman would stop by every day and buy a pretzel. Now he didn't even recognize Bruno without his cart.

"Jean-Claude's is not for me, but neither is the coffee shop," Bruno thought sadly. "Maybe lunch is not the way to become important." But then he thought about how important the man in the fine gray suit seemed, and he started getting confused. As he walked back to his pretzel cart, he thought,

"Things are not always what they seem."

Bruno didn't go anywhere for lunch for the rest of the week and David had nothing to do except to stand around and talk to Bruno.

But Bruno had little to say. Every day he became more and more quiet, especially around lunchtime and later in the afternoon, when the man in the fine gray suit came by after a lunch at Jean-Claude's. By the time Bruno got home with David, he had nothing to say and he would barely nod or grunt when Esmerelda asked him about his day.

One night Bruno was so tired that he went to bed early without his dinner. Esmerelda said to David, "Something is up with Bruno, all right."

And then David told her as much as he knew about the times Bruno went to lunch and how sad he became.

"He keeps talking about being someone and being important and I've already told him that he is important, but he just smiles and shrugs when I say that and I don't know what else to say or do," David said.

"Ah," Esmerelda said. "So that's it, is it? Well, David, you are right, of course. Bruno is important, but it is no use to tell him such things. It means nothing to him. He must be able to experience it for himself before he can believe it. I might just have an idea, David," she said softly. "In fact, I do have an idea. In fact, I have a very good idea," and saying that, she broke into a smile and said good night to David.

EIGHT

The next morning Bruno woke up with a start. Something was definitely wrong, but he didn't know what it was. Something was missing. Also, there was a great deal of noise in the hallway.

Suddenly Bruno jumped out of bed. For the first time since he was married, there was no smell of fresh pretzels in the air. He ran into the kitchen, and there Esmerelda sat, drinking a cup of tea.

"My darling," he cried. "Are you all right? Are you ill? What happened that there are no pretzels?"

"Oh, Bruno dear," she said, "I am tired of making pretzels. Today I think I shall do something else. Maybe I will read a book."

"But whoever heard of such a thing!" Bruno exclaimed. "Are you sure you are all right, my dear?"

"Of course," Esmerelda replied. "I am fine. Don't worry about a thing. You and David can do anything you want today. Walk around. Go to a movie. Everything is fine."

But Bruno wasn't so sure that everything was

fine. He took one look at David's sad face and knew that everything was not fine.

"Cheer up, David," Bruno said sadly. "Today we will do something else."

"But I don't want to do something else," David said. "I want to sell pretzels."

"But there are none today," Bruno said, looking at Esmerelda. Esmerelda said nothing at all. She just looked out the window. Bruno could not see the smile on her face.

Suddenly Bruno heard shouts from his neighbors in the hallway:

"What is wrong?"

"Where are the pretzels this morning?"

"Whoever heard of going to work without a pretzel?"

And the more they shouted, the grumpier they became. And the grumpier they became, the worse Bruno felt. When he was ready to leave, Esmerelda looked at him and said, "You look very handsome, Bruno. Have a nice day." And she gave Bruno a big kiss and pushed him and David out the door.

NINE

All that Bruno and David did all day long was walk around the streets looking at each other. David had such a sad look on his face, Bruno could scarcely stand to look at him. Every time that Bruno thought he would say something, he looked at David's face and just gave a deep sigh.

As they walked in the door that evening, Esmerelda gave Bruno a kiss and said, "My, you're home early today, dear. What a nice surprise. Is this how it will be when we have no pretzels to sell?"

Bruno gave a deep sigh and said, "I do not feel well today. I think I will go to bed." Bruno felt so sad that he fell asleep almost immediately.

Later that night, Esmerelda said to David, "I think everything is going to be all right very soon."

When Esmerelda woke Bruno up the next morning, he jumped out of bed, sure that something was missing. This time, he did not have to think.

"What," he shouted, "no pretzels again? What is the world coming to?"

"But Bruno dear," Esmerelda said, "how can

there be pretzels today when I am going to do something else? Maybe I will read another book."

Just as Esmerelda said that, there was a terrible noise in the hallway and much pounding at the door.

"What, again no pretzels!" an angry voice shouted.

"Are we to do without pretzels again?" shouted another.

"Is everybody in there crazy?" a third neighbor shouted.

"Where are the pretzels?"

The noise coming from the hallway was so loud that Bruno had to hold his hands over his ears, while David tried to hide behind the couch.

Bruno felt so sad that he sat down and started to cry. All he could think of was how much he had missed his pretzel at lunch and how unhappy he was. He looked at David trying to hide behind the couch and then at the expression on Esmerelda's face. He listened to the shouts of his neighbors in the hallway and he stopped crying.

It had never occurred to him that his selling pretzels could be important to anyone. But it was! He had only to look at Esmerelda to know that he was important to her. He was the one who went out to sell the pretzels. Without him, what would be the point of Esmerelda baking them? Didn't she say so herself, the first day they met? "I am good at baking pretzels, but not at carts." He had only to listen to his neighbors in the hallway to know he was important to them. Then he thought of all his customers who stopped by every day to buy a pretzel. Even the man in the fine gray suit who sometimes came by twice a day!

Why had he listened to the man in the fine gray suit in the first place? He had only to look at David's face to know that he had become very important to David.

Suddenly Bruno stopped feeling sad, and he jumped up and shouted, "Esmerelda! Quick, run into the kitchen and start making pretzels."

"But Bruno," she interrupted, "you…"

"There is no time for talk," Bruno said. "What is the use of trying to be someone else if it doesn't make me happy? What could be better for lunch than an Esmerelda pretzel? Everything else is nonsense.

"Oh, Esmerelda," he said, holding her. "What a fool I have been. I thought that I could become important, and wear a fine suit, too, not just be a poor pretzel vendor. I thought that you would be proud of me."

"Oh, Bruno, Bruno," Esmerelda said, "don't you

see that you are important? Listen to all these people shouting for their pretzels. You're important to them. Think of all the people who buy pretzels from you on 57th Street. You're important to them. And Bruno, to me you are the most important person in the whole world."

David came out from behind the couch and said, "Are we selling pretzels again, Bruno? That would make me very happy."

"Yes! Definitely yes!" cried Bruno.

"I must get into the kitchen and start making pretzels," Esmerelda said. "I think there will be many hungry customers today."

Epilogue

Epilogue

On the day after Esmerelda began baking pretzels again, Bruno changed the sign on his cart from BRUNO to BRUNO THE PRETZEL MAN, for even though it was obvious that he was selling pretzels— as the man in the fine gray suit had said—he wanted everyone to know how proud he was to be able to sell such wonderful pretzels, pretzels that still made his heart sing with joy.

His regular customers missed him so much that when he returned with his pretzel cart, he sold all his pretzels almost immediately.

Business became so good that Bruno had to buy a second pretzel cart. On it, he painted a big sign that said DAVID THE PRETZEL MAN.

David was very pleased to have been made a partner. Every morning he would go to the corner of Seventh Avenue and 38th Street, which is a very fine corner indeed for selling pretzels.

David likes selling pretzels from the cart and just like Bruno, he always had time to chat with his customers. And like Bruno, he always felt very important.

EDWARD E. DAVIS, born in Philadel-
phia, Pennsylvania, is a graduate of
Queens College. He lives in New Jersey
with his wife and three children, and is
the author of INTO THE DARK, published
by Atheneum. BRUNO THE PRETZEL
MAN is based on a pretzel vendor in New
York from whom Mr. Davis sometimes
buys pretzels.